caillou ®

The School Bus

Adaptation of the animated series: Marion Johnson
Illustrations: CINAR Animation; adapted by Eric Sévigny

chouette CINAR

Every morning Caillou watched for the big yellow school bus that drove down his street. He saw lots of children waiting for the bus. When it stopped outside Caillou's house, his friend Sarah got on.

Caillou saw his friend Sarah get on the bus. She said "Hi!" to the driver. The driver looked like a nice man. How Caillou wanted to ride the school bus!

Caillou asked Daddy, "When can I go on the school bus?"
"Let's see," said Daddy, looking at the calendar. "One more birthday and you'll be old enough."
That's such a long time! "I want to go on the bus now!" exclaimed Caillou.

"We can look at the bus, even if you don't ride it yet," said Daddy. "Let's go see."
The next morning, Caillou and Daddy waited for the school bus.
The driver opened the door. "Good morning, young man," he said to Caillou.

The driver's name was Mr. Washington. "This is Caillou," Daddy told him. "Next year he'll be old enough for school." "But I want to ride now!" said Caillou. "Maybe you can have a practice ride tomorrow," said Mr. Washington. "I'll ask my boss if it's all right."

All day Caillou wondered if he would get his ride
on the school bus.
He really, really hoped the answer was yes.
Caillou drew a picture. "That's me driving the school
bus," he explained.

In the morning, Caillou and Daddy met Sarah waiting for the bus. She was surprised. "Are you going on the school bus, Caillou?" The bus drove up and Mr. Washington opened the door. "Come along, young man," he said. "We don't want to be late." Caillou climbed onto the bus.

Caillou sat right behind Mr. Washington. He gave him the drawing he had made. "Now, isn't that fine?" said Mr. Washington. "I'll just tape it here on the dashboard so everyone can see it."

Riding the big yellow school bus was lots of fun! Stop. Start. Stop. Start. The bus picked up more and more children. Mr. Washington drove them all to school. At the school, the children got off – all except Caillou.

"Time to head home," said Mr. Washington.

Caillou didn't want the ride on the school bus to end. He was having too much fun!
But when he saw Daddy waiting for him, Caillou was glad to be home.

"Did you see me, Daddy?"
Daddy helped Caillou
down and hugged him.
"I sure did," said Daddy.
"Did you remember to
thank the driver?"
Caillou waved to the bus
as it pulled away.
"Thanks for the ride, Mr.
Washington!" he called.
"See you next year!"

Text adapted by Marion Johnson from the scenario of the CAILLOU
animated film series produced by CINAR Corporation (© 1997
Caillou Productions Inc., a subsidiary of CINAR Corporation).
All rights reserved.
Original story written by Matthew Cope.
Illustrations taken from the television series CAILLOU
and adapted by Eric Sévigny.
Art Direction: Monique Dupras

National Library of Canada cataloguing in publication

Johnson, Marion, 1949-
Caillou: the school bus
(Clubhouse)
For children aged 3 and up.
Co-published by: CINAR Corporation.

ISBN 2-89450-421-7

1. School buses - Juvenile literature. 2. School children -
Transportation - Juvenile literature. I. CINAR Corporation. II. Title.
III. Title: School bus. IV. Series.

LB2864.J63 2003   j371.8'72   C2003-940176-6

Legal deposit: 2003

We gratefully acknowledge the financial support
of BPIDP and SODEC for our publishing activities.

Printed in China
10 9 8 7 6 5 4 3 2 1